PRAIS
HEARTS A

★★★★

"The imaginative writing pulled me in, compelling me to finish in one sitting..."
– Tess (via Amazon)

★★★★

"Enjoyable stories for when you need a 'short, sharp, shock'!"
– Steph Ellis (via Amazon)

★★★★

"Horrifying yet well-grounded, with believable characters and settings."
– Emma K (via Goodreads)

DEMAIN PUBLISHING

Short Sharp Shocks!
Book 0: Dirty Paws - Dean M. Drinkel
Book 1: Patient K - Barbie Wilde
Book 2: The Stranger & The Ribbon – Tim Dry
Book 3: Asylum Of Shadows – Stephanie Ellis
Book 4: Monster Beach – Ritchie Valentine Smith
Book 5: Beasties & Other Stories – Martin Richmond
Book 6: Every Moon Atrocious – Emile-Louis Tomas Jouvet
Book 7: A Monster Met – Liz Tuckwell
Book 8: The Intruders & Other Stories – Jason D. Brawn
Book 9: The Other – David Youngquist
Book 10: Symphony Of Blood – Leah Crowley
Book 11: Shattered – Anthony Watson
Book 12: The Devil's Portion – Benedict J. Jones
Book 13: Cinders Of A Blind Man Who Could See – Kev Harrison
Book 14: Dulce Et Decorum Est – Dan Howarth
Book 15: Blood, Bears & Dolls – Allison Weir
Book 16: The Forest Is Hungry – Chris Stanley
Book 17: The Town That Feared Dusk – Calvin Demmer
Book 18: Night Of The Rider – Alyson Faye
Book 19: Isidora's Pawn – Erik Hofstatter
Book 20: Plain – D.T. Griffith
Book 21: Supermassive Black Mass – Matthew Davis
Book 22: Whispers Of The Sea (& Other Stories) – L. R. Bonehill
Book 23: Magic – Eric Nash
Book 24: The Plague – R.J. Meldrum
Book 25: Candy Corn – Kevin M. Folliard

Book 26: The Elixir – Lee Allen Howard
Book 27: Breaking The Habit – Yolanda Sfetsos
Book 28: Forfeit Tissue – C. C. Adams
Book 29: Crown Of Thorns – Trevor Kennedy
Book 30: The Encampment / Blood Memory – Zachary Ashford
Book 31: Dreams Of Lake Drukka / Exhumation – Mike Thorn
Book 32: Apples / Snail Trails – Russell Smeaton
Book 33: An Invitation To Darkness – Hailey Piper
Book 34: The Necessary Evils & Sick Girl – Dan Weatherer
Book 35: The Couvade – Joanna Koch
Book 36: The Camp Creeper & Other Stories – Dave Jeffery
Book 37: Flaying Sins – Ian Woodhead
Book 38: Hearts & Bones – Theresa Derwin
Book 39: The Unbeliever & The Intruder – Morgan K. Tanner
Book 40: The Coffin Walk – Richard Farren Barber
Book 41: The Straitjacket In The Woods – Kitty R. Kane
Book 42: Heart Of Stone – M. Brandon Robbins
Book 43: Bits – R.A. Busby
Book 44: Last Meal In Osaka & Other Stories – Gary Buller
Book 45: The One That Knows No Fear – Steve Stred
Book 46: The Birthday Girl & Other Stories – Christopher Beck
Book 47: Crowded House & Other Stories - S.J. Budd
Book 48: Hand To Mouth – Deborah Sheldon
Book 49: Moonlight Gunshot Mallet Flame / A Little Death – Alicia Hilton
Book 50: Dark Corners - David Charlesworth

Murder! Mystery! Mayhem!
Maggie Of My Heart – Alyson Faye
The Funeral Birds – Paula R.C. Readman
Cursed – Paul M. Feeney

Anthologies
The Darkest Battlefield – Tales Of WW1/Horror

Horror Novellas
House Of Wrax – Raven Dane
A Quiet Apocalypse – Dave Jeffery

General Fiction
Joe – Terry Grimwood
Finding Jericho – Dave Jeffery

HEARTS & BONES
BY THERESA DERWIN

A SHORT SHARP SHOCKS! BOOK

BOOK 38

© Demain 2019 / 2020

COPYRIGHT INFORMATION

Entire contents copyright © 2019 / 2020 Theresa Derwin / Demain Publishing

Cover © 2020 Adrian Baldwin

First Published 2019

All rights reserved. No part of this publication may be reproduced, stored or transmitted in any form or by any means, electronic, mechanical, photocopying, recording, scanning or otherwise without written permission from the publisher. It is illegal to copy this book, post it to a website or distribute it by any other means without permission.

What follows is entirely a work of fiction. The names, characters and incidents portrayed in it are the work of the author's imagination. Any resemblance to actual persons, living or dead, events or localities is entirely co-incidental.

Theresa Derwin asserts the moral right to be identified as the author of this work in its totality.

Designations used by companies to distinguish their products are often claimed as trademarks. All brand names and product names used in this book and on its cover are trade names, service marks, trademarks and registered trademarks of their respective owners. The publishers and the book are not associated with any product or vendor mentioned in this book. None of the companies within the book have endorsed the book.

For further information, please visit:

WEB: www.demainpublishing.com
TWITTER: @DemainPubUk
FACEBOOK: Demain Publishing
INSTAGRAM: demainpublishing

(*Fruit Of The Womb* originally appeared in "12 Dark Days" ed. Dean M. Drinkel for Nocturnicorn Press 2017)

CONTENTS

DORIS	**9**
FRUIT OF THE WOMB	**27**
BIOGRAPHY	**57**
ADRIAN BALDWIN (COVER ARTIST)	**58**
DEMAIN PUBLISHING	**61**

DORIS

Birmingham—The End
When the apocalypse started and the world went to shit, at least I had Doris, an abandoned dog I'd adopted. She was my best friend, really. As small as I am tall, sweet, and a real cutie.

We only walked outside during the smog-heavy day, around what's left of this building site of a planet. We wouldn't venture out at night, oh no. It was far too dark and anyway, that's when *they* liked to come out.

I used to talk as we walked in the weak sunshine and Doris always listened. I often ranted about how we got here. Humanity's fault. Mum grew up in the '70s with all of those nuclear bomb scares and emergency evac practices at school. She showed me old footage and told me how they used to like scares, 'cause they got a half hour outside in the sun, in the playground.

The *constant rain* started around my sixteenth birthday. Just at the turn of the year 2000, when loads of people were predicting the end of the world—*again*.

I was raised in the Midlands with decent, if poor, parents. I saw enough TV to be scared when things got real. It started slow, insidious. A public election, a debate posted all over the Internet, then an unpopular winner. Well, unpopular to the *sane*, that is.

Of course, when the war started and one in a long line of celebrities-turned-president decided to press the button, I wasn't surprised.

So there I was, having survived the bombs, the clouds, and the degradation of nature, fighting for survival—alone.

Alone until I found Doris. I'd even managed to avoid the onset of numerous diseases, which spread to the UK in the aftermath of the bombings. I wandered the streets of a desolated city with Doris by my side, searching for scraps of food.

Most of the corner shops and bigger supermarkets had been raided months ago, and my stash was mostly gone, so I had no choice but to leave our little hidey-hole in an old Wetherspoon's pub in the centre of Birmingham and head outside.

I heard the noise first; an odd, chittering sound, hissing, clacking, clicking of mandibles against each other. Tiny claws dancing on the rubble as they, too, searched for food. They were close by—the Chitterings. God, I hated those unnatural fuckers.

***

How The Church Took Over

I don't know who first called them 'Chitterings', but it stuck.

On reflection, I remember hearing about them on the radio after the shelters were opened. Of all the things to survive, it was the bloody cockroaches. They had got bigger from the environment somehow, and were now the size of small rats. They had some sort of bugs on them that were dangerous. And they *liked* to bite.

The Renewed Church of Survival had warned us about them, the few of us who were left. The Church controlled the only radio station; it aired at set times during the day, with an obligatory mass service during the evening. It was the only bloody entertainment we had apart from the decrepit books I'd found on the old wooden shelves in the pub.

From what I understood about the Church, a few of the bigger cathedrals or the monumental churches had hidden panic rooms below the foundations, and a few priests, nuns, and select VIPs had been given expensive tickets to the bunkers.

They'd been fed, watered, trained in survival, a few had died.

And the remnants of the Catholic Church emerged with a brand new plan, weapons and food.

At first, I'd been in Birmingham when the world died, and with my family dead, I had nothing but the *Church*.

Once they'd emerged from those panic rooms, they became kind of like the Salvation Army, they'd raided every government building, every supermarket, every abandoned home, 'acquiring' supplies and holding them under one roof.

They were utilising Birmingham Cathedral at the time, right in the centre of the city; an old, stone building with stained-glass windows, surrounded by dead grass and a circle of mausoleums.

They had outposts in St Basil's and St Chad's a half mile or so away, but those areas were more dangerous to travel to at night.

When the food in *my* empty rental house ran out, and all the other lodgers had fled, I was starving for human contact more than actual protein. I left my gross floral, peach wallpapered bedroom in the morning, and joined the queue of the homeless, the lonely and the lost, outside the cathedral.

Or, as they'd renamed it with a big sign scribbled in red marker; *The Renewed Church of Survival.*

I didn't know who came up with the new branding, and I didn't care as long as I had people to talk to, and a little food.

The only way to survive apparently, was to pray and to work.

I did wonder at the time; if they really believed that, then why the armed guards?

Of course I found out 'why', pretty quickly, when a Chittering cluster started hunting for food at the St Basil's centre.

Bullets sorted them out quick enough.

***

Before The End

The animals were the first to sense the end coming; once the bombs fell and destruction reigned, they let their fear be known.

We could all hear barking, howling, other screams of denial and fear, late into the night as we attempted to regroup, save what we could.

Most of the cats and dogs fled or starved. I didn't want to think what it would be like to be a pet like a mouse, a guinea pig or a bird, trapped in a gilded cage forever. The animals were the sensible ones; rats deserting a sinking ship of a planet. We humans, we huddled in the dark, waiting for help to come.

I first met Doris, a beautiful cockapoo, at one of the refugee camps in Warwick before it all got disorganised and the food ran out. Before I retraced my steps and returned to Birmingham. Animals weren't a priority, so there she was, slumped in a corner of the camp, skinny little thing. And I fell in love instantly.

I was taking a quick, sneaky fag from my last stash, standing near the cinderblock barriers that surrounded Warwick castle, a massive fortress thirty-five miles from Birmingham. Built in yellow, beige and grey brick, the intimidating towers were a weird shape. It was everything I remembered, and it was a perfect refuge. It must've been formidable a few centuries ago.

It'd taken me about a week to get here from the flat I'd been renting in an old Victorian three-storey house, walking most of the way. It was thanks to me hiding in that dingy, cold flat for a week that I'd survived. No one knew I existed so no one came to hurt me, pillage my goods, or worse.

The whole world had gone insane, like Black Friday in America—people running around with makeshift weapons robbing food, petrol, tools, and TVs. The urgent supplies I understood, but TVs? *Really?*

Once I'd emerged into debris strewn streets, littered with the charcoaled, twisted bodies of the remnants of humanity, I knew I had to leave. Especially when the smell started making me hungry. Fire was the easiest way to get rid of any lingering diseases once a person had died.

Of all the people I expected to meet on the street, Mad Malik had been bottom of the list. But still, it was the bipolar Indian guy—the guy my Dad used to call a nutter, who would hop from bus to bus, dancing as he rode—who yelled "castle" as he danced along the street to soundless music.

I stopped him, asking him to repeat what he'd said.

"Castle—War castle where they've all gone."

"War? Yeah, there was a war—"

"Naaa, go war."

It took me a moment to figure out what he meant, and then the name struck me: *Warwick.* I'd gone there with my Nan when I was a kid. It was cheap to get to on the coach, cause it wasn't far.

"*Who* Malik? Who's gone to the castle?"

"Guns!"

Then Malik turned away from me, his hands holding his useless headphones tightly to block out the sound of my voice.

The sound of everything.

The army. *Nice one!*

That's when I started walking, hitching, trading fags and anything else I had in my crappy rucksack, for thirty-plus miles of roads 'til I got to the Warwick base camp.

***

Warwick—Meeting Doris

I took a drag, breathing in the sweet death of tobacco, really not giving a shit at this stage if cancer took over. There were worse ways to die now. I'd heard stories...

I don't know why Doris trusted me from the off; maybe because I, too, was bedraggled and half-starved.

My knees cracked as I lowered myself down, hand held out, palm up, in supplication.

"Hey there, little one," I whispered, voice high and lilting.

She whined, tucked her head down, and tried to avoid eye contact.

What the hell had happened to her? Who'd done this? Made her so scared?

She had a pink, diamanté studded collar on her, with a leash.

"Hey girl, c'mere," I tried again.

Her cute fluffy ears pricked up, she raised her head, and two deep hazel eyes met mine.

"Yeah, come on," I said, still holding my hand out.

I used my left hand to rummage in the pocket of my duster, 'til I found what I was looking for. Half a packet of digestive biscuits; my day's ration, but this puppy needed them as much as I did. Maybe more.

I took a biscuit out, held it towards her.

Slowly, she shuffled closer, sniffing. I broke up the digestive biscuits into crumbs, but I'm sure more of it went onto the floor than in her mouth.

She showed her appreciation anyway, with a flick of her tongue on my cheek as I bent further down, touching hard limbs and matted hair. Her tongue was cold and surprisingly hard for a dog, but I supposed it was being left out on her own for so long with very little water that had made it so rough.

I laughed and started ruffling her neck, then her skinny frame started running in circles, chasing her own tail, before jumping up on me, her dirty paws resting on my knees as she licked my face, this time with more enthusiasm, making me laugh out loud.

It was the best *wash* I'd had in ages. Though I use that term loosely.

"Good girl," I said, dropping a kiss on her head and cuddling her, "come on, I'll look after ya."

I took the pink leash and slowly walked her towards my sleeping bag.

Or at least, that was the idea.

I didn't get very far.

The armed guards stopped me before I got through the barbed-wire barrier. The few elderly or disabled who'd survived, plus the really young kids, got to stay inside the old building. But the rest of us, we stayed outside on the burnt-yellow remnants of grass.

Still, I let out a huge sigh of relief as I crossed the barricaded area into the main encampment; the muddy grounds of the castle sucking my boots down as I trudged back toward my sleeping bag, where the healthier and younger of us were scattered around in tents, black bags, sleeping bags, blankets or old newspapers. Whatever we could find.

I tugged the pink leash along, dragging Doris with me.

What was left of the military had cordoned off the main hall of the castle and were using it for planning and strategy.

It was dinner by the time I got back to my area, so I tucked Doris—that's what I'd decided to call her 'cause she reminded me of Nan with those big hazel eyes—into my sleeping bag, grabbed my old tin bowl, like we used to use on school camping trips, and headed for the 'mess'.

The food, cooked up by a huge guy in dirty fatigues and an even dirtier apron, wasn't much to speak of, but who was I to argue? We were all starving, fighting for survival after a nuclear winter, and had little choice.

So, beans *à la carte* it was.

I took my meagre helping with resignation, grabbed some left over Ryvita crackers that'd survived the storms, and went back outside into the cold evening air.

The camp area outside the castle building was scattered with dirty sleeping bags, makeshift tents put together from cardboard, old newspapers and rags.

It was starting to turn cold, and we all sat, in our tiny areas, huddled together for warmth.

I could smell faeces, piss and the pungent tang of clothing that hadn't been washed in months.

We were the new 'homeless'. Ragbags of humanity, frozen limbs clinging desperately to each other.

It was killing me.

I'd come here for human contact, but this wasn't it.

This was degradation and hell.

I left a few days later and headed back to my home town.

Malik had survived, maybe there were others.

***

Birmingham—The Chitterings And The End

After our return to my hometown, I'd been lucky enough to find a small entrance into The Dirty Swan, an old pub in the town centre that had already been pillaged, so was no longer of interest to anyone.

But we had to be careful all the same.

I hid in one of the booths, clutching Doris. I had to be as quiet as possible. I prayed that Doris would be quiet, but she was as good as gold and didn't make a sound.

Every day, other than playing that damn radio, we were silent as thieves.

A few days after I'd settled me and Doris in there, we needed food. So, out we went.

I'd wrapped myself up in an old tarp I'd found in the cellar. It hindered my movements a bit, making me clumsy, but my coat by then had turned into fragments.

I hoped that it would offer at least some protection.

We were rooting through a bin; the smell wafting up my nose more like putrescence and piss than anything. But you never knew where you'd find something useful.

My rummaging was interrupted by a noise behind me, and I spun round.

I *knew* that noise.

Fuck.

I turned towards the Chittering, its mandibles clacking, me brandishing a makeshift weapon I'd made from an old-style beer pump made of black wood and brass, yelling at Doris to get behind me.

She ignored me of course.

At first she was static; frozen in fear maybe.

"Doris, move!"

She remained still.

I didn't know what had gotten into her.

What happened next is a bit of a blur, but I thought I saw Doris dart forward. Two feet high and full of rage, honey-brown fur glinting in what was left of the sun, she ran at the beast, a deep growl in her throat.

I screamed as her teeth penetrated the hard shell of the insect. I heard the sharp fracture, and a hiss from the creature, then tried to hit the damn thing with my weapon, but couldn't catch it without hitting Doris too.

It was then I fell, suddenly dizzy, the ground smacking me as I landed on top of the creature.

I rolled instantly, nursing a swollen wrist.

I sat, stunned, watching fur and insect fly, scrapping their way across the dead ground, until at last I heard my Doris yelp, then whimper.

I whispered in sympathy.

My wrist was throbbing by now.

Must've fractured or sprained it, I thought.

Doris scampered towards me, favouring one leg, and I scooped her up in my arms, ignoring the flash of pain in that wrist, cooing at her gently. "It'll be alright Doris, it'll be okay."

She was licking her paw as I held her; a futile attempt to sanitise the already-spreading blood and pus.

"Shit!"

Doris whimpered again and I felt myself tear up, my throat tight, my pulse racing.

I couldn't lose her.

I just couldn't.

She was all I had left.

***

One Last Phone Call

"Nan, nan! Can ya hear me?"

"Just about luv, it's so loud here."

I remember the last time I spoke to Nan, before first the internet then the phone lines disappeared.

I'd been glued to the TV, watching a bright buffoon of a man bluster his way through excuses until he spoke the words we feared the most.

"We are at war!" he'd declared.

I sat alone in my flat, in the three-storey building, my arms wrapped around me in a self-hug, fear gripping my chest.

This was it then.

What the hell was I going to do?

I could go see the people in the flat downstairs, talk to them.

But it wasn't the twentieth century anymore.

Neighbours didn't talk to each other.

They sat glued to the 'box' watching the inane antics of has-been celebrities trying to scrimp a living by eating bugs in a jungle.

Kind of ironic really, considering the circumstances.

At least they'd probably survive the aftermath.

It hit me then, for the first time.

I was alone.

Really *alone*.

So I did the only thing I could do, and called Nan.

"*Nan, nan! Can ya hear me?*"

"Just about luv, it's so loud here."

So loud everywhere.

Sirens erupted, warning signals.

Then my mobile winked out of existence and I started to cry, sniffling down the now useless phone, desperate to hear her voice before the end.

***

You Can Look Now—This Really Is The End

I shuffled as quickly as I could, back to our home at the old pub in Birmingham, holding Doris in my arms, cooing to her, telling her it'd be alright even as I cried messy tears over her fur.

Should've stayed at the camp, I thought. But they'd been bullying me about Doris, teasing me for adopting a helpless animal in the middle of the apocalypse—for valuing something more than food. And the hopelessness of the refugees had crippled me.

"Shhh, 's'okay hun, we'll be inside soon, you'll be fine."

I didn't believe it.

But I had to make *her* believe it, or she'd give up.

I got her inside through the cellar of the pub and crawled up through the back amidst empty boxes and barrels. Once in our little booth, I lay her on the worn, burgundy seat.

I looked at the open wound, seeping yellow pus; the smell of rot crashing over me like a tidal wave.

I felt sick, dizzy.

Dying, I realised.

What was the point?

We'd screwed up a world we should've nurtured, and we'd killed ourselves.

"Doris," I said, holding onto the taut pink leash, "I'm sorry hun. Should've stayed at the castle. But I couldn't fight the arseholes anymore, you know?"

Her hazel eyes, once wide and bright, were tired and threaded with hints of yellow, kind of like my own.

"I couldn't, Doris."

"I know," she said.

I climbed up onto the seat in our booth, next to her, wrapped my arms around her frail, hard body, hugging her for all I was worth.

Hard body?

How had I not noticed it before?

The stiff frame, her empty eyes, the little wheels in red supporting the white scooter Doris was attached to.

The hard leash, a handle intended for young children to drag their 'pet' along on 'walkies'.

The smell of decay was nearly overwhelming by now, the pain in my wrist blocking everything else out.

I could hear the Chitterings outside the door, the little bastards waiting for me to die so they could feast.

I turned on the radio to listen to The Renewed Church of Survival give the latest sermon on foraging and 'Ten Ways With Beans'.

At least it drowned out the sound of the creatures scratching at the door.

FRUIT OF THE WOMB

Jay sighed as he pushed his overburdened shopping trolley up the aisle of his local supermarket, moving back his mop of straggly dark hair, partially hidden under a black woolly hat. His back was causing him jip gain, and his gaze inadvertently wandered towards the alcohol section. Not that he was tempted when he didn't drink anymore 'cause of the painkillers.

£2.99 for a two litre plastic bottle of cheap shit cider. Were they taking the piss? What chance did the independent brewers like him have? Distilling cider and perry at small farms, hoping tourists or loyal customers stopped by to—*well*—buy.

It was a tough industry and it was getting tougher every day with the whole Brexit thing kicking off last year and the pound turning to nothing. And as for his crop; fuck all. The weather had all but destroyed it. He blamed climate change, if that's what it really was. Himself, he reckoned it was the government—poisoning the air with all those chemicals. And they did it on purpose. Forcing small businesses to fold so the big supermarkets kept all the profits and they took a share. Bastards. But they'd have to get up early in the morning to catch him out. He'd show 'em.

He pushed his trolley up to the shortest (ten items or less) queue and started unloading his shopping onto the conveyer belts. After a minute or so the grouchy looking old lady at the till with the bad perm pursed her lips at him in disapproval.

"You know this is the 'ten items or less' aisle? You're at thirteen things now."

Inside, where she couldn't see, he grinned.

"Er, oh sorry, didn't see," he said, snickering to himself when he got away with it. She'd already rung up most of it and it was easier for her to carry on. So begrudgingly she did. Another result for 'Team Jay'.

He handed over lots of crumpled vouchers to knock the amount down by 75p then his credit card.

He hissed and gritted his teeth as she tapped his card on the EFT unit and the LCD screen flashed 'DECLINED'. He'd used the contact-less a few too many times and some of it had gone through already. Bollocks.

"Er, sorry," he mumbled, words barely intelligible as he rummaged in his wallet for his last and best hope, "try this one."

She zipped it across the device.

He let out a breath as the words "TRANSACTION APPROVED" appeared.

Thank fuck, for this time at least he thought, packing essentials into the few wrinkled 'bags for life' he'd carted around since the robbing bastards started charging 5p for a carrier bag.

Groaning, he lifted his bags and half shambled, half trotted out of the supermarket onto the village high street and by-passed the few local shops; an actual butchers for one, a florist, a pound shop, and a card and gift shop selling candles and crap.

Jay heaved himself through the large oak doors of an old 17th century pub, The Dog and Partridge.

The old wooden sign hanging from the front showed a wolf-like dog tearing out the throat of a brown and grey partridge, blood spattering the worn image, the gilt frame equally worn and tarnished.

Once inside he scanned the lounge looking for a free table, ignoring the sudden silence that seemed to fall as he entered. Stares from the locals and the gruff red-headed barman met his gaze. He nodded once to acknowledge the looks.

Fuck me, it's the Slaughtered Lamb, he thought, to rid himself of the uncomfortable trickle of sweat and fear that crawled down his aching spine.

If it weren't for the *welcome* he'd received he'd have liked the pub; oldy-worldly varnished oak tables scattered around the lounge, scuffed from years of use and the ghosts of previous clientele, beer mats strewn across each table, the room itself infused with an amber glow from the faux Victorian gas lamps the lit the area.

The top half of the walls, above a border rail, were painted a deep red; *not maroon*, he thought, or blood red, or crimson. Something in between—that was it. The colour was *carmine*. It made the lounge seem that little but darker. The wall below the border was decorated in old fashioned cream and red flock wallpaper.

Each wall was scattered with traditional prints or paintings.

The only thing missing was one of those 'dog playing poker' prints.

The very room had an earthy, musty aroma, clinging to the walls.

Behind the large, L shaped bar stood the barman, impressively solid, with tattooed muscles shown through a t-shirt printed with the image of the dead partridge. *Nice.*

Said barman, who looked positively Celtic with a beard Thor would envy, grunted as a Jay approached.

Jay dropped his bags on the sticky, beer-coated floor and let out a sigh of relief.

"Get ya?" the barman growled.

"Er, pint of Coke."

No *please* from Jay. He was used to asking and getting. So he was surprised when the barman muttered "*Seriously?*"

"What?" Jay replied brusquely.

He hadn't noticed the barman pour something while he was dropping his bags on the floor.

Instead of the drink he'd requested, a ceramic partridge shaped mug appeared on the counter before him. He'd been messing about on his phone and hadn't noticed the tap the barman poured from.

"You come in 'ere," the barman said, "you 'ave our special brew. No excuses, mate."

Bloody hell, he really had entered *The Slaughtered Lamb*, he thought, eyeing up the mug.

"I'm on tablets," he muttered.

"Won't kill ya," came the nonchalant reply.

He huffed, about to tear the bloke a new arsehole, or complain as usual, ask to speak to the manager or something, then thought better of it.

Bloke was big, moody looking.

Giving in he picked up the mug and brought it up tentatively towards his nose and sniffed.

"What is it? Lager? Bitter?"

"Ale, mate," the guy snickered.

Fucking dick.

"Yeah, yeah, okay," he said, finally risking a sip.

It was weird. Weren't half bad though, he reckoned. Bit malty, tangy and a bit flat now he thought about it. He hadn't had a beer in ages, but even he could tell it was too flat.

"Mate, ya beer's gone off. It's flat."

The barman had the cheek to burst out laughing.

"Hey!" Jay said.

"'Old on, 'old your horses. Sorry, didn't mean to laf. It's meant to be flat. From the barrel, mate."

"Oh ah, got ya. Sorry. Ok, what's the damage?"

Damn, second sip in and he was starting to enjoy it, a warmth and strange mellow feeling suffusing him. Couldn't even drink his own perry; not without getting addicted or binging, but this beer, well, he was pretty sure he could drink it all day without a problem.

Hell. It might even help with pain better than the stuff the bloody doc gave him.

"How much?" he grunted, putting the brown ceramic mug back on the bar.

"Now," the barman said with a sly smile, "that's a whole other conversation if you're after a little help with your business as well mate. Are ya?"

Jay put down the mug hard, a smidgen of beer spilling over the edges.

"What?!"

The red-head leaned in, almost intimately, his ruddy, bearded face mere inches away from him.

The homophobe in Jay was suddenly worried he might try and snog him, and edged backward.

"Not inclined that way, mate," the guy said, reading Jay's discomfort. "Look, take a pew, give me five secs, then I'll be over with an—interesting—proposition for ya."

Flummoxed, Jay nodded silently, grabbed the ceramic mug of beer and ambled over to the table he'd spotted earlier, first leaning down with a hiss of pain to grab his carrier bags.

True to his word, the tattooed giant came over to where Jay sat, carrying his own mug of beer, and a pint ceramic jug, which he used to top up Jay's beer.

"Right, first things first," the bloke said, taking a slug of his own beer then holding out his large hand for Jay to shake.

"I'm Attis."

Weird name, Jay thought absently.

"James. People call me Jay."

Jay shook the offered paw nervously, the other hand swallowing his, then took a swig of his own beer, again relishing the moment of pain relief it offered.

"S'nice stuff you got 'ere," he mumbled between another mouthful.

"Sure is Jay. Make it meself."

"Yeah?"

"Yeah."

"Where you from?" he then asked, assuming Ireland or Scotland 'cause of his colouring.

"Originally Greece," Attis answered, surprising Jay, "but—I get around. Don't stay in one place for long. But when I'm travelling I like to help people."

Ahh, there it is. Tit for tat. What's he after?

"Help 'em how?" Jay prompted, pissed off with the pussy-footing around, eager to get to the important bit. Cost.

That was the core of his personality; nothing for free in this world, gotta pay. And Jay didn't want to pay if he could avoid it.

That's why his pear crop was dying and this year's perry was shite. He hadn't been willing to pay for the oils and treatments required to get rid of the infestation of pear psylla. Little bastards had all but destroyed his pear orchard, laying eggs, secreting the honeydew and attracting ants. Apart from the ants it sounded harmless; honeydew. More like larvae sperm if you asked Jay.

"A little bird tells me you're having problems with your crop this year, well, I know some—technique—that can help."

Jay was immediately suspicious.

"I thought we was talking about this beer."

"Oh we are," Attis said, "that's all part of the package I can offer."

"I'm listening," he grumbled, watching eagerly as Attis refilled his mug from the seemingly endless jug of beer.

***

The advert appeared in the corner shop, newsagent and pub window the next day.

> *Pear tasters wanted*
> *Turton Perry Farm*
> *Albarton*
> *Worcester*
> *Call Jay on 97892 429 716*

"You seen this, babe?"

Ashli wandered up to Kyle, a broad guy in his thirties, who was looking in the shop window at the adverts, where a hand scrawled scrap of paper had caught his eye.

"What is it?"

Ashli came behind her fiancé, wrapping one arm around his waist.

They'd been hiking, stopping in pubs and B&Bs for a week now, exploring most of Herefordshire.

"Ooh!" Ashli gasped, reading the sign Kyle had indicated, "is that what I think it is? Free cider?"

Kyle turned into her, his hands rubbing up and down her pink, bare arms.

They'd been lucky so far, only one torrential downpour in England was pretty lucky as far as Kyle was concerned, the rest of their trip blessed with sunshine warm enough that they were both wearing shorts and t-shirts.

"Yep, sorta," he answered, dropping a light kiss on her forehead, "perry. Same stuff but made outa pears instead."

Another "ooh," from Ashli who offered Kyle a delighted smile.

"Go on then, shall we do it?"

"Yeah, go on then," she answered, grinning.

"Nice one."

Kyle let go of Ashli, grabbed his phone and took a quick picture ten put his phone back in his pocket.

"Pub?" he suggested.

Ashli agreed and they ambled over to the local pub, The Dog and Partridge, ignored the weird stares they got and found a table in a corner, grabbing the menus.

Kyle looked down at his growing belly with dismay, uhmed and ahhed over the salads, then thought *stuff it*.

"I'm 'aving pie and chips," he said, "looks good. It's got their local beer in the gravy."

"Cool. I might as well have that myself," Ashli responded, having scanned the menu and decided they were on holiday, so what was a few more pounds on the hips between friends?

"Sure?"

"Yeah."

Kyle grabbed his wallet out of his rucksack and headed up the bar, where a red-headed barman, who looked kind of like a character from *Vikings* or *Game of Thrones*, stood waiting, cloth in his hand as he polished the counter.

"Hi," Kyle said, nodding at the barman, "we're in that corner there," he said, gesturing, then placed their food and drink order, deciding they should both try the local beer, and chatted to the amiable barman for five minutes, asking him for directions to Turton Perry Farm.

Kyle came back to the table, carrying two brown mugs, grinning like an idiot. Ashli figured he'd already sampled the local beer. They were gonna be *so* drunk by the night-time.

Ten minutes later the barman turned up with their food and cutlery.

"Spoke to Jay," he said, no preamble, "he's grabbing his van and picking you up in about an hour. Says you can bunk in his barn if you want. He's got an inflatable air bed."

"Really?"

"Kyle!"

"What?" Kyle asked, turning to his fiancé.

Ashli smiled up at the barman.

"Can we get back to you after our food please?" she asked, "I just need to run something by Kyle."

"Sure enough," the barman said, "you need me—ask for Attis."

He headed back behind his bar, collecting empties along the way and Ashli let out a huff of frustration.

"Are you nuts?" she hissed, leaning in to Kyle.

Kyle looked at her, eyes wide, oblivious.

"What?!"

"We don't know anything about this bloke. Could be a nutty psycho farmer who shags his sheep or something."

Kyle spat his drink, a fountain of ale, sputtering with laughter.

When he finally stopped coughing, tears were streaming from his eyes and he grabbed a napkin to wipe his face.

"We're not in Wales, babe," he finally said with a cheeky smile, "now eat your grub before it gets cold."

Ashli signed, grabbed her cutlery and started eating.

"Okay, but only if you reckon it'll be alright," she said.

"Yeah, it'll be *cool*," he reassured her, tucking into his own pie and chips, "don't worry, babe, it'll be fine."

***

Attis sat at a table chatting to one of the old fellas who frequented the pub; the old guy was flicking through the local paper and sipping a pint.

Attis supped from one of the partridge shaped ceramic mugs, enjoying the brief high it gave him. In his hands he held a small, dark brown, leather skinned book, the pages yellow with age and musty.

He was taking a risk investing in Jay.

He was hoping it would pay off.

Just as long as the idiot remembered the correct incantation.

"Hi, *Attis*?"

The tourist—Kyle, he recalled—stood near Attis' table with his curvy, brunette girlfriend.

"Yep, that's it, what can I do ya for?"

Kyle's feet shuffled, a little uncomfortably.

"We decided to take you up on that offer if it isn't too late," he asked hesitantly.

The girl, Ashli if he got it right, stood next to Kyle, shapely but pale legs on display.

He took a second or two to enjoy the sight, his gaze travelling up and down her figure.

He saw her shift a little behind her boyfriend so he grinned, then stood up and took Kyle's hand to shake in his firm grip.

"That's great," Attis said, "you two sit here, I'll send Marian over with a coupla refills on the house and I'll get on the blower to Jay. You'll have a blast, trust me. You'll never forget it, as long as you live."

***

By the time he sent them outside to sit on the bench, the tourist couple were a little squiffy—he'd made sure of that—and the sun was starting to set.

As they climbed into Jay's scratched, red van, circa 1982, Attis waved them away cheerfully, but not before handing the old leather-bound book to Jay through the driver's side window.

"Thanks a lot for this," Kyle said, trying to hold his elbows in to avoid knocking the farmer who was driving.

"No worries," Jay said, "you and the missus are doing me a favour."

"Great."

From there they all sat in relatively uncomfortable silence, all of them squashed up too close to each other, making it difficult to move.

When they finally drove up a narrow, gravelly country road, with plenty of trees clustered around, blocking out the sun, Ashli started to jiggle nervously in her seat, causing Kyle to glance at her questioningly.

Finally they emerged into a clearing, and she let out a relieved breath as it became clear that it was, indeed, a farm of some sort.

Jay clambered out of the van first, with an oomph sound, favouring his left leg.

Then he opened the passenger side door, offering Ashli a hand to step down.

She took it reluctantly.

She supposed he looked normal for a farmer; scruffy, bulky, casual. But he still gave her the creeps for some reason.

Kyle on the other hand didn't seem to think there was anything off about him, judging by the look he threw Ashli.

Stretching her legs she scanned the farm, and Jay took the opportunity to point out what was there.

There was a fallow field, barren and dead.

Rows and rows of pear trees, the fruit glistening in the evening light.

An odd, sickly sweet scent hung in the air. She figured it was the sheer amount of the overripe fruit.

In one corner was a large barn, and a Jay indicated that's where they'd be sleeping that night.

It housed his small brewery area apparently, full of large vats and smaller barrels filled with variations of the perry they'd be sampling.

Down another gravelly path was a cottage-style house; tatty, unkempt, like its owner she thought.

"Right then," he said, gesturing towards the house, "grab a seat on me sofa in there while I make some sarnies, or cheese and biscuits for you to have as your tea. Yeah?"

"Yeah," Ashli replied.

"Great." Kyle's response was much more enthusiastic.

Heaving their rucksacks from the back of the van, they followed Jay through the tiny hallway into his house, veering to the left and taking a seat beside each other on the low, worn, dark chintz two-seater.

"Cuppa?" Jay asked, dropping his carrier bags on an old pine table they could see in the kitchen he'd just walked into.

"No thanks," said in unison this time.

Ashli might be a little uneasy, her perv-radar going off, but she figured he was probably harmless.

The last beer she'd had at the pub, the local brew the Viking had given her, had made her feel a little more relaxed.

Must be stronger than the Pinot she normally had.

Whilst their sullen-looking host made a flask of tea and the sandwiches, Ashli dug through her smaller rucksack, dodging make up and underwear, grasping her mobile phone and holding it up at various angles trying to get a signal.

No chance.

"Crap," she muttered, showing Kyle the one bar and 'no signal' status.

"Don't worry so much," he said, throwing his arm around her, "you can call your mom tomorrow—when we *finally* get up," he added, laughing.

"Okay, sorry. I just like to let Mom know what we're up to."

Kyle pulled his fiancé close into him, kissing her softly on her forehead.

"You're just like her," he said, "you worry too much, babe."

"Ready, you two?"

Both looked up to see Jay's bulk hovering above them.

"Yeah," they both answered, finally in agreement.

Jay moved back, another crappy carrier bag in his hand, this one filled with sandwiches, a tin cup and his flask of tea, and they stood up.

"Follow me," Jay grunted.

Twenty minutes later, they were all sat in the barn on upturned old barrels for seats, Jay sipping a mug of tea, the food laid out on an old crate, utilised as a make-shift table, straw everywhere, and behind them the massive vats he showed them and selection of smaller barrels, six or so, labelled with their contents.

The sickly, over-sweet smell permeated the air.

It must be part of the Perry distilling process, Ashli reckoned.

Despite the weird aroma, she was definitely beginning to enjoy herself.

Jay was basically plying them with different varieties of Perry in large plastic cups, and they were on their second already.

Truth be known she was already pretty sozzled, and they were all laughing, Jay being quite entertaining by this stage, sharing stories of the complaints he'd made to loads of companies in order to get refunds or freebies. He was kind of like a Del Boy farmer.

The last thing she remembered before getting even woozier, then passing out, was Kyle murmuring her name then falling unconscious from the barrel to the straw-strewn ground.

***

"*Ash, Ash?*" Kyle mumbled, voice croaky, thirst attacking him before he'd even opened his eyes.

And he had tried to open them but the felt like they were glued together.

Damn, his head was banging and when his eyes finally opened, his vision was still blurry.

Then the extreme thirst hit him, throat so dry and sore it was as if he were stuck in the desert.

Serious hangover, he thought, struggling to move his arms and push his legs up from where he sat, so he could get up and grab a drink.

So thirsty.

Maybe it was man-flu and not a hangover.

Where was he? Where was Ashli?

He tried calling her name again, but all he got for his troubles was a harsh garbled whisper.

Slowly, the blurriness subsided and he looked around to get his bearings before attempting to get up again.

The barn.

Vats of perry; empty barrels they must've drunk dry.

And Jay standing above him, with that carrier bag of his, grinning like a fool.

"Jay? Give us a hand up?" he rasped.

Jay laughed, dropping his bag on the floor, then muttered "that stuff in the Perry was good. 'Ave to use it again."

"*What?*"

Kyle to tried to move his arms again, realised he couldn't then looked left, then right, then let out a whine of panic.

His arms were held out, horizontal, tied crucifix-style to a bar, and they were bruised.

Whimpering, not knowing what the fuck was going on, he looked down at his torso, scratched and bloodied, and below, his dick was free, his bare legs lying stretched out on the ground where he sat.

Both ankles were tied down with rope, attached to a forklift truck he'd vaguely seen last night in the barn.

A ragged scream escaped him as he started to struggle, legs first, then arms, panic engulfing him, drenching his body in sweat.

"*What the fuck*?!"

"Shut up," Jay said.

"Let me go, lemme go. *Ash*!!"

"I said SHUT THE FUCK UP!" Jay screamed at him, now bending down at the knees, his face inches away from Kyle's.

"Please, please, where's Ash?"

"If you shut the fuck up you'll see," Jay snarled, eyes narrowed, one hand clenching and unclenching again in anger, or frustration. Kyle didn't know, but he mumbled "yu…yeah," snot running down his nose, and kept quiet. And as still as possible.

Please god let her be okay, please let her be alive.

"Stay here. I'll go get the missus," Jay said, standing up.

He turned his back on Kyle and walked out of the barn, a slight limp on his left leg, and Kyle was frozen for a moment as tried to get his head around what the hell was going on.

Stay here. Was he fucking serious?

Kyle started pulling at the ropes that bound him, letting out a raw, hoarse scream, part pain, part fear.

His pulse was racing, head thudding, and his wrists and ankles chafed as he fought desperately to get untied.

He was aware he'd started crying as he saw a figure walk into the barn through blurred eyes, and he stopped struggling, watching, panic almost consuming him until he recognised Ashli, bare footed but wearing some kind of slip-dress in white, her hair straggly, arms bound in front of her.

She was fighting, pulling against Jay who walked a couple of feet behind her.

As she stopped in front of Kyle she groaned through a dirty gag, sank to her knees, breasts heaving. Kyle saw the wire hoop fastened around her neck.

"Babe," he wheezed, heart breaking as he saw the loop was attached to some kind of rod and Jay held the handle.

He was treating her like cattle.

"Please, let her go," he croaked, staring up at the farmer.

"I told you to shut up," Jay mumbled, "and I brought the slut to see you."

Kyle opened his mouth to rip him a new arsehole, started struggling then Ashli wheezed trying to tear at her neck.

Jay had tightened the wire.

Kyle closed his mouth, kept still.

He shut the fuck up, like he'd been told to do.

"What—whaddaya want?" he whispered at last, when Jay seemed calmer.

"You, sit!" Jay said, pulling once on the rod he held for emphasis.

Ashli obediently fell to the side and onto her bum at Kyle's feet, tears streaming down her face.

"Shh," Kyle whispered.

Jay let go of the rod in his hand, letting it drop to the floor but Ashli didn't move, didn't try to escape, just sat there rocking, arms held tight against her chest.

She'd seen this coming. She'd known. How had his baby known?

Jay leaned down and was rummaging through the carrier bag that looked like it had been used a million times, then stood up holding a bottle of water, and something hidden in his hand.

He walked round Ashli, who still sat there and rocked back and forth, mumbling to herself through the gag.

Kyle tried to sink further into the floor as Jay knelt down beside him and opened his hand revealing a large blue pill.

He grasped Kyle's jaw and forced his mouth open shoving the pill in.

Kyle started squirming and shaking his head side to side, as Jay's large hand started to crush his jawbone, then a scream erupted from his mouth and the bottle was at his lips, water filling his mouth, at once blissful, yet frightening.

"Swallow."

He tried to fight the instinct but he couldn't and before he could stop it the pill went down his throat, Jay had pulled the bottle of liquid gold away, dropping it on the sawdust floor, and stood back up, moving back to Ashli, who froze, a deer caught in headlights, as he grabbed the end of the rod again.

What the fuck had he taken? Drugs? Poison? Oh god just let Ashli be okay.

He lay there for five minutes, fear a bomb waiting to explode in his chest, but nothing happened, no dizziness, nothing.

Until—

He frowned in confusion as a familiar sensation started in his balls, then in his dick.

He gasped, eyes widening in surprise as his penis began to swell, the pulse of excitement tugging in his groin, his balls and his dick, which he looked down at, literally stunned as it grew and hardened until it was fully erect and his scrotum ached with need.

Oh god, oh god, he needed. He needed—

Sex.

What had he taken?

His breathing was getting faster now, until he was positively panting, his hips moving up and down, then he groaned, part pleasure, part intense pain.

All confusion.

He knew he was thrusting but he couldn't stop himself.

It felt so wrong but so fucking good.

"What—did—you—do?" he gasped, glaring at Jay, desperately fighting the arousal that coursed through him.

Jay laughed.

"Viagra mate, you'll thank me later."

What the Fuck!

"Right, you're ready."

Jay pulled at the rod, tipping Ashli over onto the ground. Then, placing his arms under her armpits he heaved her up, and threw her down, face flat on top of Kyle, 'til the couple's lips would've touched if it weren't for the gag.

"Girly, fuck your boyfriend—now."

Kyle's eyes, less than an inch from Ashli's, widened in sudden understanding.

She'd said he was some sort of perv. She was right.

He wanted to watch.

If they gave him what he wanted, he might let them go.

Hope sprang inside him and he stared straight at the woman he loved.

"Do it, babe. Ashli. Do it, it's okay. It'll be okay, I promise."

She grunted in acknowledgment, their heads too close to nod.

Groaning with the effort, she wiggled her hips further down Kyle's body, until her opening met his dick.

She writhed, trying to push herself back up, away from him so she could assume what had been their favourite position.

Her on top.

Sensing her predicament Jay tutted and hauled her up, then dangled her until she used her bound hands to put Kyle's dick inside, then kneeled, legs spread on either side of his bound legs.

She screamed through the gag as she forced herself harder, pushing down on top of his groin, the pain a sharp knife as her unprepared body took him inside.

Kyle was thrusting eagerly by this point, unable to stop himself.

***

Grinning, Jay leaned down to the carrier bag, taking out the brown, leather book Attis had passed him through the car window just yesterday. And a ceramic statue of a bird.

A 'Vuçedol' Attis had called it. Some sort of deity.

He put it on the ground at the bottom of Kyle's twitching feet.

He stared at the couple fucking, his own dick unresponsive.

This was just a job after all.

His crop was dying, he had to make the land fertile again, and Attis had shown him the way.

"This is for you mate, Er, Attis," he said, opening the book and reading the jumble of foreign words out loud.

Just as he spoke the last of the ritual, Kyle screamed, coming, his body buckling, and Jay quickly grabbed the last thing from the carrier bag and darted to where Kyle's head banged against the bar which held his arms tied tight.

"Not yet," he yelled, kneeling at the guy's head, bringing the rusty blade to his throats and slicing across, before standing back up and wiping the knife on his trousers.

Blood spurted from the slash in Kyle's neck, his entire body thrashing, eyes rolling back in his head.

The girl scrambled backwards screaming and keening hysterically through the gag, all the way through the bloke's death throws.

"Nice one," Jay muttered, putting everything back in the carrier bag, picking up the end of the rod and dragging the girl backwards.

"All done for now," he reassured her, finally giving up on the rod, dropping it and pulling Ashli to her feet.

By now she was sobbing uncontrollably, half dragged, half stumbling along with a Jay as he led her towards his house then dumped her on the sofa, where she started rocking to and fro again.

"Cuppa?" he asked, putting the kettle on, not waiting for her to try and answer through the gag, "gotta get you warm. But you can't have no more of me Perry."

Ashli continued to rock, empty, alone.

"Attis wouldn't like it if you lost the baby."

She didn't hear him, could only hear the thumping of her heart, the drumming in her ears, her own keening wails, and Kyle's gurgling screams as he took his last breath.

BIOGRAPHY

HWA member Theresa Derwin writes Urban Fantasy, Horror and Horror Erotica, with over fifty anthology acceptances, one in 'Below the Stairs' with Clive Barker, Ramsey Campbell and Paul Kane.

She is in her first year MA Creative Writing at BCU.

When she became too ill to work, she accepted medical release, to pursue a writing career. As well as physical disabilities she has cognitive function issues, and writing gives her an escape from her illnesses.

She's had four collections published; has edited over nine anthologies. Her forthcoming books include *God's Vengeance* from CLP and collection *Sex, Slugs and Sausage Rolls*.

She is the 2019 HWA Mary Shelley Scholarship recipient.

She blogs at www.theresaderwin.co.uk
Twitter @BarbarellaFem

ADRIAN BALDWIN (COVER ARTIST)

Adrian is a Mancunian now living and working in Wales. Back in the 1990s, he wrote for various TV shows/personalities: Smith & Jones, Clive Anderson, Brian Conley, Paul McKenna, Hale & Pace, Rory Bremner (and a few others). Wooo, get him! Since then, he has written three screenplays—one of which received generous financial backing from the Film Agency for Wales. Then along came the global recession which kicked the UK Film industry in the nuts. What a bummer! Not to be outdone, he turned to novel writing—which had always been his real dream—and, in particular, a genre he feels is often overlooked; a genre he has always been a fan of: Dark Comedy (sometimes referred to as Horror's weird cousin). *Barnacle Brat* (a dark comedy for grown-ups), his first novel won Indie Novel of the Year 2016 award; his second novel *Stanley Mccloud Must Die!* (more dark comedy for grown-ups) published in 2016 and his third: *The Snowman And The Scarecrow* (another dark comedy for grown-ups) published in 2018. Adrian Baldwin has also written and published a number of dark comedy short stories. He designs book covers too—not just for his own books but for a growing number of publishers. For more information on the award-winning author, check out: https://adrianbaldwin.info/

DEMAIN PUBLISHING

To keep up to-date on all news DEMAIN (including future submission calls and releases) you can follow us in a number of ways:

BLOG:
www.demainpublishingblog.weebly.com

TWITTER:
@DemainPubUk

FACEBOOK PAGE:
Demain Publishing

INSTAGRAM:
demainpublishing

Printed in Poland
by Amazon Fulfillment
Poland Sp. z o.o., Wrocław